BAREFOOT BOOKS

The barefoot child symbolizes the human being whose natural integrity and capacity for

action are unimpaired. In this spirit, Barefoot Books publishes new and traditional myths,

legends and fairy tales whose themes demonstrate the pitfalls and dangers that surround

our passage through life; the qualities that are needed to face and overcome these dangers;

and the equal importance of action and reflection in doing so. Our intention is to present

stories from a wide range of cultures in such a way as to delight and inspire readers of all

ages while honoring the tradition from which the story has been inherited.

THE
CRANE'S GIFT

A Japanese folk tale retold by
S T E V E & M E G U M I
B I D D L E

Illustrations by
M E G U M I B I D D L E

B A R E F O O T B O O K S
B O S T O N & B A T H

Barefoot Books, Inc.

the children's book division of

Shambhala Publications, Inc.

Horticultural Hall

300 Massachusetts Avenue

Boston, Massachusetts 02115

Graphic Design by Design/Section

Printed in Belgium by Proost International Book Production

This book has been printed on 100% acid-free paper

Biddle, Steve

The crane's gift: a Japanese folktale/retold by Steve and Megumi Biddle;

illustrations by Megumi Biddle.

p. cm.

Summary: After he rescues a crane one cold winter night in the mountains of northern Japan, an
old man and his wife are visited by a mysterious young woman who stays with them almost a
year before they discover her true identity.

ISBN 1–56957–932–6 (acid-free paper)

[1. Folklore—Japan.] I. Biddle, Megumi. II. Title.

PZ8.1.B526Cr 1994

398.24'52831—dc20

94–7573

CIP

AC

T his story belongs to northern Japan, where every winter the beautiful landscape is covered with a harsh blanket of snow. One of the visitors that adorns this snowy winter climate is the Tancho crane. This beautiful bird is notable for its pure white feathers, elegant form and graceful, dance-like motion. In every-one's heart, the Tancho crane is regarded as a symbol of long life, peace and happiness.

Long, long ago, deep in the mountains of northern Japan, there lived an old married couple. They were poor as poor can be, but they were simple, kind and gentle folk. Everyone near and far knew them for their honesty, the love they had for each other, and their deep respect for every living creature.

Even though they were both very happy with their life, sometimes they did feel a little lonely. They often thought about what it could be like if they had a child of their very own, especially a daughter.

Every day the old man would go into the mountains and gather wood, which he would burn into charcoal. About once a month he would go to town and sell the charcoal that he had made. In this way he managed to make a living for himself and his wife.

Into the old couple's mountain landscape winter would come with a burst of silky white that draped the whole world for miles around in a thick insulating quilt of snow. The sky was covered over with dark, heavy curtains of cloud that shut out all the colors and flavors of the previous seasons.

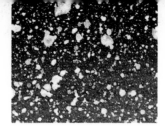

One dark, freezing winter's evening, when the snow was falling heavily and the chilly wind was blowing ever colder and stronger, the old man was returning home from town, tired and exhausted after a long day selling his charcoal to the townspeople. Shivering with cold as he trudged along the mountain path that would take him to his wife and a nice warm fire, he suddenly heard the harsh, painful cry of a bird in distress.

"Where can that sound be coming from?" thought the old man to himself.

Peering through the curtain of ever-falling snow, he caught sight of a hunter's trap, in which a beautiful white crane was caught. The more the crane struggled to be free, the tighter the trap became entwined around its leg. It was very obvious to the old man that the crane could not escape and fly away to freedom.

"Oh, you poor bird! If somebody should find you in this condition, they would surely catch you," said the old man softly, as he made his way toward the crane. He then got down on his knees and began to open the trap.

"Please do not fret. I have come to help you. Your leg seems to be injured just a little," said the old man, with love and tenderness in his voice.

The crane, seeming to understand what the old man was saying, stood quite still. As if to comfort him, it placed its head against his cheek, and made warm, peaceful sounds of happiness.

Once the crane was freed from the trap, it flapped its wings, ran forward, and flew off into the snowy sky. As it flew up high, the crane turned its head around as if to take one final look at the old man. In doing so, it uttered a loud cry.

"Thank you," the old man thought it meant.

The crane sailed in a circle three times over his head, and then finally flew away. The old man looked up into the snowy sky and watched the crane get smaller, until it had completely disappeared into the distance, high above the mountains.

The snow was cold and the wind was strong, but the old man felt a strange warm feeling in his heart.

"This is how everyone must feel after they have done a good deed," he thought to himself. He knew that he had done a good deed by saving the crane's life and this made him feel very happy. *stop*

That same evening, sitting by the warm fire, the old man told his wife of the good deed that he had performed.

"How peaceful and full of happiness the crane looked!" he said.

Then they spent the rest of the evening idly talking about his day in town and about the people he had met there. They were just about to go to bed, when there was a loud knock at the door.

"Who would come to visit us on such a terrible night as this?" asked the old woman. "Husband, please go and see who could be there on this cold and snowy evening."

The old man made his way to the door and opened it. There, to his amazement, stood a beautiful young lady. She was dressed in a glorious white silk kimono. Her hair was black and flowed right down to the middle of her back. The texture of her skin was a smooth as a piece of polished white porcelain.

Megumi Biddle

"Very sorry to trouble you kind people," she said in a very gentle voice. "I am on my way to visit my relations who live in the next town. But I seem to have lost my way in this terrible snowstorm. Could you let me stay with you for just one night?"

As she stood in the doorway, a soft and tender smile appeared on her lips. The old man and his wife could see that she was shivering and that her delicate hands were trembling because it was so cold.

"Please! Do come inside, child, and warm yourself by our fire," said the old man, taking pity upon her. "We do not mind you staying here for one night."

"You can stay with us for as long as you like," added the old woman as a token of friendship.

"Thank you very much for your kind offer of hospitality. Do you really mean that I can stay as long as I like?" asked the young lady as she brushed the snow off her clothes and wiped her feet.

"Then it is settled," said the old man. "You can stay as long as you like."

"Come over to the fire; dry your clothes," continued his wife. "We can talk more in the morning after we have all had a good night's sleep."

The next day it snowed so heavily that it was impossible to open the door. The snow kept falling for five or six days, and the young lady stayed on, wondering all the while how she could repay the old couple for their kindness toward her.

"There is a request I would like to make of you," she said to the old man and woman.

She seemed to pause. The old couple, who now felt that she was like a daughter to them, encouraged her to speak.

"Please do tell us," they said. "Is it anything we can do to help you in any way?"

The young lady began to tell them of how she had lost her parents, and how on that evening, when she had knocked on their door, she had been on her way to stay with some relations who lived in the next town. But she had lost her way in the snowstorm.

Then she continued, "They could never take the place of my parents like you have. It must have been some kind of good deed that has brought me to your house. Could I possibly stay here and be your daughter?"

"How lonely you must be without your parents," said the old couple. "You are such a kind and understanding young lady. It would make us both very happy if you became our daughter."

So, with these kind words, the young lady stayed on and became the daughter that they had never had. Little did she know how happy her request had made them.

It was when winter had turned into spring, and the flowers on the cherry trees had transformed the whole countryside into a sea of pink blossoms, that the young lady made another request of the old man.

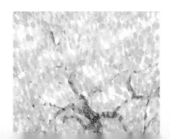

"Do you have a loom in the house? I should like to do some weaving."

"Yes, there is one," said the old man. "There is a loom that my wife used to weave cloth on when she was young."

So saying, he took her into a workroom where they had stored the loom and many boxes filled with spools of colored thread.

The young lady then said to the old man, "I have a very important request to make of you. Please promise me that you and your wife will never open the door to the workroom while I am at the loom and weaving."

The old man promised her that they would never look. All the same, he thought it was a strange thing to be asked.

"Please leave me now and close the door behind you," she kindly asked him.

The young lady worked from morning until night, never resting or eating. From behind the closed door the old man and woman listened to the rhythmic sound of the loom as it went *creak, tap, clack…creak, tap, clack…creak, tap, clack…*

It was on the fourth day after the young lady had started weaving that the sound of the loom suddenly stopped. Before the old couple had even a second to think about what had happened, she appeared in the doorway. In her hands she was carrying a roll of cloth.

"What beautiful cloth!" they exclaimed. "We have never in all our married life seen anything like it before."

"I have made it for you," she said. "Please take it to town tomorrow and sell it, for I am sure it will fetch a good price for you."

The next day the old man went to town, and shouted, "Cloth! Cloth! Who will buy my beautiful cloth?"

Everyone to whom the old man showed the cloth was amazed by its quality and workmanship.

One of the townspeople who saw the cloth said, "Old man! This is not just cloth but brocade. It is the most ornamental brocade that I have ever seen in my whole life! Why, we must go together and take it to the castle so that the lord might have a look at it."

Upon seeing the exquisite brocade, the lord exclaimed, "This is indeed most beautiful! With this cloth I will be able to have a truly stunning kimono made for my daughter. Let me buy it from you."

With these gracious words, the lord gave the old man a large sum of money in gold coins.

Then he added, "Please do come again. Your cloth is of such great beauty that I will buy all you can bring me."

As soon as the old man got home, he told his wife and the young lady how he had been able to sell the cloth to the lord for a very good price.

Spring had now turned into the wet heat of summer. The rainy season had transformed the whole countryside into a patchwork of color, from the refreshing blues and pinks of the morning glories to the intense blues and purples of the irises and hydrangeas.

However, the young lady was quite unaware of the change of season, as she was working from morning until night, never resting or eating. From behind the closed door the old man and woman once again listened to the rhythmic sound of the loom as it went *creak, tap, clack…creak, tap, clack…creak, tap, clack…*

In their mind's eye the old couple could see every detail of the workroom as they imagined the young lady sitting at the loom. It was very hard for them to resist the temptation to look inside and watch her at work, as they were very curious as to how she could weave such beautiful brocade. But the old man always remembered the promise that he had made to her, that they would never look inside the workroom while she was weaving.

After many days, she appeared in the doorway looking a little exhausted and very pale. But in her hands she was holding a brocade that was even more beautiful that the one she had previously woven. The old man took it to town and showed it to the lord.

The lord was so pleased with the brocade that he bought it from the old man, paying him a larger sum of money than before.

As the old man was about the leave, the lord said, "Old man, toward the end of the summer my daughter will be getting married. Would it be at all possible to commission a special brocade from you for her wedding kimono?" The old man was more than happy to agree to such a request.

With the money they received from the lord, the old man and woman became richer, and life became easier for them. But with the passing of each day, the young lady grew paler and thinner, losing all of the energy that she once had.

The old man, who was worried about the young lady, said to her one day: "Do you not feel well? You must be working very hard, weaving day and night. Please do have some rest."

"Oh, I am all right," she replied with a warm smile. "Really, I only want to weave a little more cloth. But I have a request to make of you. Please promise me once again that you and your wife will never open the door to the workroom while I am at the loom and weaving."

The old man promised once again that they would not disturb her while she worked. All the same, just like last time, he thought it was a strange request.

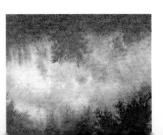

Megumi Biddle

That night, when he and his wife were sitting by the fire, the old man expressed his concern about the young lady's health.

"I am worried about her too," agreed his wife. "Just listen to the sound of the loom. It seems to be saying, this work is hard! This work is hard!" Walking towards the workroom, she said, "Shall I take a look inside?"

"No," replied the old man. "Please remember the promise that I have just repeated to her, that we will never look into the workroom while she is working."

But the old woman was insistent, "Just a peep. She will never know."

So saying, she went outside and slid back the workroom window. Looking inside, she let out a soft cry of amazement.

"What's the matter?" asked the old man as he hurried outside. "What do you see?"

"It's a…" replied the old woman, lost for words.

The old man was also lost for words as he looked into the workroom. Because sitting at the loom, where the young lady should have sat, was a slender white crane. As they both watched, the bird bent its head down and with its beak plucked out one of its own feathers, which it then carefully wove into the yarn.

"The young lady is a crane," said the old man very softly. "Look! She is using her own feathers to make that beautiful cloth. Can you see those bare spots on her body where she has pulled out the feathers?"

The old man and woman quietly slid the window shut and tiptoed away. They were both full of wonder and amazement about what they had just seen.

The following evening the young lady appeared in the doorway, looking very exhausted and extremely pale. But in her hands she was holding the most exquisite brocade.

"Please accept this as a final token of my love and respect for you," she said, sitting down in front of the old couple. "As you were requested by the lord, I have woven this brocade for his daughter's wedding kimono."

The old man and woman were lost for words. They could only think about the sight that they had witnessed the previous night.

The young lady continued, "I would like to thank you for all that you have done for me during the last few months, for the time has come for me to return to my family."

Tears were now flowing down the old man's cheeks. As he turned to look at his wife, he noticed that she was crying as well.

"Old man," the young lady continued, taking his hand as if to comfort him, "I am the crane that you set free from the trap that snowy winter's night. Somehow I wanted to express my gratitude to you. So I changed myself into a young lady. To help repay you, I wove the brocade. But last night you both broke your promise to me and discovered my secret. Now I cannot stay here any longer. I must fly south before the winter arrives."

With a sad backward glance at the old couple, the young lady dashed out of the house. As she ran, she stretched out her arms and instantly transformed herself into a white crane. With a flap of her wings, the crane flew up into the sky.

"Goodbye, and thank you for all your help," the old man and woman called after her.

The crane flew in a circle three times over their heads. Just as on that first winter's evening, she turned her head around as if to have one final look at the old couple. In doing so, the crane uttered a loud cry.

"Goodbye, and thank you," they both thought it meant.

They watched the crane get smaller and smaller, until she finally disappeared into a sky reddened by the glow of the setting sun.

Megumi Biddle

It was when the bright hues of summer had turned into the warm earthy colors of autumn, and the air was clear and crisp, ripening the harvest and sending the birds south, that the old man and woman happened to look up into the evening sky. Seeing a lonely crane flying overhead, they could not help but wonder if it was their young lady...